THE TEACHER AND THE VIRGIN

THE VIRGIN PACT - BOOK 1

JESSA JAMES

GET A FREE BOOK!

Join my mailing list to be the first to know of new releases, free books, special prices and other author giveaways.

http://freehotcontemporary.com

The Teacher and the Virgin: Copyright © 2018 by Jessa James

ISBN: 978-1-7959-0195-6

All Rights Reserved. No part of this book may be reproduced or transmitted in any form or by any means, electrical, digital or mechanical including but not limited to photocopying, recording, scanning or by any type of data storage and retrieval system without express, written permission from the author.

Published by Jessa James
James, Jessa
Teacher and the Virgin

Cover design copyright 2017 by Jessa James, Author
Images/Photo Credit: Stocksy: Viktor Solomin

Publisher's Note:

This book was written for an adult audience. The book may contain explicit sexual content. Sexual activities included in this book are strictly fantasies intended for adults and any activities or risks taken by fictional characters within the story are neither endorsed nor encouraged by the author or publisher.

1

ane

"*Who?*" the note read.

I turned my head to the right and met my friend Anne's curious green eyes. She raised an eyebrow up at me, remaining quiet. There was no talking in class, but I immediately knew what she was asking. Words weren't needed. Not for this.

Who was I planning to lose my virginity to?

Anne and I, and eight other girls in the senior class, made a pact to lose our virginity by the end of summer. Graduation was next week, so we had a couple months to get the deed done before we all went off to college. All of us being eighteen, we'd felt it was past time, especially since going to an all girls' school made near impossible to find worthy boys. We wanted to go to college *experienced*.

I didn't want to be the last virgin in our group, but I didn't have to worry. I didn't have to find a *boy* I liked. I didn't have to pretend to be in love, or chase after some stranger at the mall. I knew *exactly* who I wanted to get naked with.

I wanted Mr. Parker to take my virginity. I wanted my teacher to punch my V card.

Mr. Parker. He was only a few years older than me, and not skinny and awkward like the guys my age. No, he was *all* man.

While I saw him every day for my US government class, I doubted he noticed me. I was just one of his many students. One more young woman in an endless see of long hair and cherry flavored lip gloss. I existed in an ocean of khaki and plaid, the school's overly conservative uniform. Underneath, I wore a lace bra and matching g-string panties every other day, the days I had Mr. Parker's class.

And before class, I went to the ladies room and took off the bra. I loved the way my heavy cotton shirt rubbed my sensitive nipples, and I hoped he'd notice the hard tips that ached for his touch.

He was gorgeous and educated, his hard ass and broad shoulders made my innocent body squirm. I didn't want to be innocent, not when I was around

The Teacher and the Virgin

him. I wanted to be naughty, but I doubted he noticed me.

But I noticed him. Every inch of his well-muscled form.

Yeah, he was the one who I was going to give myself to. I had no idea how, but it was going to happen.

He was gorgeous, dark hair that was overly long for the rules of the private school. He wore a tie to please the principal, but the knot was always loose, as if he hadn't the time to get completely dressed. I spent most of the class fantasizing about all the ways he could tie me up with that long strand of silk and turn me into a real woman.

"Ladies, I know it's the last day of classes before exams, so we're going to do a review on everything the final exam will cover. Colleges still look at final grades." His deep voice made me shiver and I couldn't stop staring at the muscles in his neck. I wanted to taste him. Which was weird, but I couldn't stop imagining kissing him…all over.

I wasn't worried about the final exam. This was the one class I was getting an A in, the one class where I always paid attention. How could I not stare at Mr. Parker for the entire hour? If the other girls thought I was gawking at the hot teacher, what did I care? They gawked, too. I couldn't keep her eyes of the flexing muscles in his forearms. He rolled up the sleeves of his dress shirts to write on the board, and I always had to go back and read what he wrote after. I couldn't stop staring at his hands.

Even Molly seemed hypnotized when he moved, and I was pretty sure she was a lesbian.

He was *that* hot. But none of the other girls would have him. No. If he was going to have one of us, if he was going to take a young, virgin pussy, then it was going to be mine.

I spent the entire year watching his ass as he walked back and forth lecturing. I studied the veins in the back of his hand as he wrote on the board. I studied his mouth and wondered what his lips would feel like against mine.

When the bell rang at the end of every class, I left the room with wet panties and hard nipples.

His class was the best part of my day. I even raised my hand to answer questions and preened when he smiled at me when I gave the correct answer. I wanted to please him, which was another odd sensation for me. I wasn't a people-pleaser. But for Mr. Parker? Well, I wasn't quite sure where I would draw the line, but I wanted to find out.

With Anne's note in my hand, I stared up at Mr. Parker from my seat in the third row. He was trying to be stern, but he was probably just as ready to be done for the summer as we were. The school was small, one of those girls' prep schools for rich parents who wanted a sheltered education for their privileged daughters. Yes, we always got teased about the usual stereotype, how we were crazy, spoiled, entitled brats with issues. The school had kept me from boys my age, which is what my parents wanted, but their plan backfired. It put me in front of the one man I craved.

Yes, I wanted a man.

I didn't want to be fucked by a boy who had no clue what he was doing. I wanted Mr. Parker.

Oh yes. I shifted in my chair, trying to ease the ache in my pussy at the thought of him filling me up. I wanted him to take my cherry, to split me wide open—his cock would be big—and he'd do it right.

While he continued to talk about the three branches of government, his smooth velvety voice only made dark carnal thoughts, wild fantasies, fill my mind.

"Fuck me," I'd tell him, glancing at the desk just behind him.

Yes, the desk. I fantasized about that desk almost as much as I did Mr. Parker. I was no longer the good student, but one who'd been bad. Very bad.

I'd be bent over his hard desk with my plaid uniform skirt barely hiding my ass. I'd have had to undo the top few buttons of my prim white shirt so he could see that I wasn't wearing a bra, my nipples tightening as they touched the cold wood.

A shiver would run down my spine when his finger grazed my lace panties. I would feel the heat pool there, making the damp fabric cling to my folds.

"You've been a naughty girl, haven't you?" the familiar velvety voice would say. His breath would warm my neck as he leaned over me, dominating me. I'd squeeze my legs together to try and ease the growing ache, but it wouldn't work. The press of his hand against the lips of my pussy would have me crying out.

"You're just wearing a thong in my class and no bra." His voice would be a mix of shock and mischief, and I would no doubt blush as he reached around and cupped an exposed breast.

Teachers weren't supposed to behave this way, I'd think, even as his other hand would come down on my ass in a harsh swat. They weren't supposed to reprimand naughty schoolgirls over their desks, but I would wiggle my hips because I'd want the spanking he'd give. I'd push my pert bottom out for more, for anything he'd give me.

"Do you know what happens to girls when they're naughty?" he'd ask.

"They get punished."

"That's right," he breathed against my neck. "But you're extra naughty, so you'll get my hand instead of the ruler. I want to make sure I can feel every single count."

Nothing about the way Mr. Parker would look at me would be soft. He would be like a beast with its prey. His look would be hungry, with me the answer to quenching his thirst. I would shiver again when his finger started to rub painfully, slowly against the gusset

The Teacher and the Virgin

of my thong. His other hand would start to move against my ass cheeks, my bare flesh available for him.

"After your ass is nice and red, then you'll show me that you're a good girl again and suck my cock. Nice and deep." He would rub a finger over me, slip the tip just inside my virgin heat as he held me in place over his desk. "And then I'm going to taste your naughty pussy and make you come."

I moaned at the thought of him teaching me exactly how he liked it, of him dominating me, making me his. The mangled sound stirred me from my fantasy. I shifted in my seat again, trying to rub my thighs against my swollen clit.

All around me were my classmates, but they seemed not to notice the sound I'd made just *thinking* about Mr. Parker.

While he was the Civics and Government teacher in this small, private school, he'd finished law school last year and was studying for the bar exam. Being a teacher wasn't his career, like the other teachers who'd been at the school for decades. He was on the fast track to becoming a lawyer. He should have been stiff and stodgy; all the teachers were. Safe even, but nothing about the way he stared at me spelled "safe."

Sometimes, I imagined that he stared, that his gaze traced the curve of my leg or lingered on my lips. I dreamed that he wanted me, masturbated in his shower thinking about taking me over his desk. I dreamed that he couldn't control himself when it came to me, that I was so beautiful, so perfect that he couldn't say no.

No imagination needed on my end. I definitely wouldn't say no.

Mr. Parker was nine years older than I was – *yes, I stalked him* – and a man of that age had years of experience I could only dream about. That easily spelled trouble for me, but I wasn't running away from it. I wanted him and if I had to be punished because of it, I was fine with that, as long as Mr. Parker was doing the punishing.

Anne was writing something down on a piece of paper while the others worked on a practice test and whispered about what they were doing over the summer. I couldn't care less.

Why would I, when the only thing I wanted was standing right in front of me?

I spun around when another piece of paper hit my head. Anne raised and lowered her eyebrows at me. I realized my imagination had run wild again. I should've known better. Having almost-sex with Mr. Parker would *never* happen in real life. I saw him every day in class, and he'd never want anything to do with me. I was his student and too young. Yes, I was eighteen, but still...

The whole situation was hopeless. A man like him wanted a woman, not a girl. He would want woman who was experienced and worldly and didn't look like a lost puppy with a leash around its neck. I tried to brush the thought aside. It made me sad because I couldn't be alluring and experienced unless I fucked someone else and the only one I wanted was him.

I tried as best as I could to not think about it anymore, as I smoothed out the paper Anne had thrown.

"You're undressing our teacher with your eyes. Don't deny."

"Shut up". I quickly scribbled down before I passed the note back to Anne. She passed it back seconds later.

"Mr. Parker's too old."

I bit my bottom lip. That was exactly why he was so attractive; I got hot for an older man. I got hot for *him* and I quickly wrote my thoughts down.

"I bet he knows what to do with his c—"

I hesitated writing the last word. I was getting wet just thinking about writing a fucking four-letter word. It shouldn't have been a big deal – writing down the word "cock". What was I getting so worked up over? My classmates reading the note? Or worse, Mr. Parker?

Cock. Cock. Cock.

Cock. Cock. Cock.

See, I could say the word in my mind over and over again. Why couldn't I just write the damn thing down?

Cock. Cock. Cock.

Oh, God. My tongue definitely needed to be drowned in holy water.

"I bet he knows what to do with his cock." I quickly

passed the note, letting out a sigh of relief that I finally wrote the damn word down.

Jane – 1. Cock – 0.

"You're crazy. He's a teacher. You'll be a virgin forever. He'll never touch you."

I pursed my lips when I read Anne's note. I didn't want to admit it, but the note stung, especially since I'd graduate next week and never see him again. It hurt because it was true. There was no way someone as gorgeous, smart, and experienced as Mr. Parker would want anything to do with an eighteen-year old Catholic school girl whose only sexual experience was with her own hand. I really was a virgin in all aspects, and the cold, harsh truth started to sink in.

How was I going to lose my virginity if I didn't know the first thing about sex? Sure, I knew how to pleasure myself and some porn videos seemed easy enough to follow, but would the real thing be as easy to do? The only dicks I'd seen in person were my cousins' back when our parents would make us swim naked together when we were four years old. I was a cold, lonely—and horny—virgin.

"We graduate in a week." I passed the note to Anne, bit my lip.

Now, I was just writing down random things in the hopes that she wouldn't see right through me and realize how affected I was by what she'd just said.

"He'll never touch you."

It stung, really. I'd been crushing hard on Mr.

Parker since the start of the school year and now it was almost over. What would I do when I couldn't see him every day?

"He's hot."

"You ARE crazy. There's no way you're having sex with a teacher."

My reply to her was easy, and the truth. *"I don't want anyone else. He's the one who's going to take my virginity."*

Making it happen was impossible.

My jaw dropped to the floor when I saw Mr. Parker walking towards me. *Was my deepest fantasy finally coming true?* Of course not. Before I knew it, he took the notes in my hands and skimmed through them.

Oh. My. God.

I glanced at Anne and her cheeks were as red as her hair. She hadn't been the one who'd written all those things in the notes. She wasn't the one who was going to be in trouble. I was.

This was the perfect time for the floor to open and swallow me whole. This would be social suicide – my classmates finding out I wanted to fuck my teacher. Telling Anne in a note was one thing, but this? God, I'd never live it down.

I didn't even want to think about what my parents would say when I was sent to the office. They were absent most, if not all the time, and only seemed to care when it was to reprimand or ground me. I spent about half the school year living with the maid as they travelled Europe, or Africa, or wherever the hell they were now. Knowing I wanted to have sex with a teacher would make them freak.

I closed my eyes and waited for him to read it aloud like he usually did when he caught us passing notes.

Holding my breath, I looked up at him through my lashes.

His dark eyes were pinned to mine as he read the note. "Can't wait to be done with school. No more uniforms," he said, his voice loud for all to hear as he walked back to the front of the room.

I whipped my head up when those words came out of his mouth. He read it, knew the truth and didn't give me away?

I was safe from my classmates, but not from him. The way he looked at me curiously was a dead giveaway. I couldn't read him though, and it was freaking me out and exciting me at the same time. He knew how much I wanted him now. He *knew!* But he looked emotionless. Was he disgusted or infuriated? Was he even shocked, or was this a common occurrence with his students? Would he send me to the principal's office? Did he think the note was a joke? Or worse? Did he think it was real and just had absolutely no interest? Maybe he had a smoking hot model for a girlfriend, someone who knew her way around his cock, who knew how to please him.

I didn't know anything about what to do with a man. All I knew was I wanted him.

He raised his brow, and the blush that surfaced on

my cheeks was automatic. Thankfully, the bell rang, and Anne and I stood up from our seats in a rush. I grabbed Anne by the arm and almost ran towards the door. I was almost free from further humiliation until I heard my name being called.

"Jane," said that ever-familiar voice that haunted my imagination. When my friend stopped to stand beside me, he added, "You can go ahead, Anne. I just want to have a word with Jane."

The rest of my classmates filed out of the room and Anne followed suit. When it was finally just the two of us, I clasped my hands together and waited for the sermon. I wanted to hug myself. No good could come out of my teacher reading a note basically saying I wanted him to fuck me. Was thinking dirty thoughts enough for disciplinary action? Could I be expelled? My heart sunk. Graduation was next week. There was no way—

He crossed his arms over his broad chest. "I want you right here, one hour after graduation."

I didn't want to overthink more than what I was already doing, but the way he looked at me made it seem that I had nothing to worry about. Instead, I had *everything* to worry about. I waited for him to say something more and watched as his eyes trailed from my ankle socks, up to my plaid skirt to my white blouse, then finally met my surprised gaze.

Did he know I was wet for him? Could he see me squirming from his scrutiny?

I never got the answer to that. When an unfamiliar student entered the room, that was my cue to leave and head to my next class.

"Jane, you didn't answer me," he said.

"Yes," I replied, starting toward the door.

"Yes, *sir*," he added and I stopped in my tracks.

A shiver coursed through me at the deep tone of his voice.

I glanced back, saw that he was waiting for me to repeat it.

"Yes, sir," I whispered, finding saying those two words really hot. Yes, I wanted him to be my teacher in more than just US government.

As I walked the hallways I'd never see again in a week's time, all I could think about was after graduation. He'd told—no, commanded—me to come back and meet him. I just had to wonder… why?

2

*M*r. Parker

SHE WAS FUCKING GORGEOUS AS SHE RECEIVED HER diploma, and she knew it.

With wavy blonde hair that fell past her shoulders and deep brown eyes, she was so damn hot.

Jane. *My Jane.*

The high school was small, only a few hundred students. So even the teachers were in the loop when it came to students, even if they didn't have a student in their class. I knew Jane was one of the most popular senior girls. It was easily because of her looks. She had soft and welcoming facial features, but her body… *Oh, fucking hell.*

The black graduation gown hid her lush curves, but

I had every single one memorized. I'd spent the entire year imagining her ass beneath that plaid uniform, knowing her pale skin would turn a bright pink when I spanked it.

I had to pause and think about fucking baseball stats to will my dick down. Getting hard in an open field just at the exact moment graduation ended only spelled trouble. The older academics would balk at the sight of me, and the parents, who thought so highly of the institution, would call the police if they saw one of the teachers getting hard staring at the graduating class.

But I wasn't looking at the entire class. I only cared about *her*.

My Jane.

She was the girl every other female hated and wanted to be and the one guys wanted fuck. I balled my hand into a fist when I felt my blood start to boil. Just the thought of boys her age wanting to fuck Jane made me want to break or punch something. I got riled every time I heard about a senior party, about all the cute boys they'd met. Had some idiot got to touch Jane's pert breasts? Had they parted her creamy thighs and filled that tight pussy? Had they spurted all over her in their adolescent haste and left her unfulfilled?

A deep growl had the music teacher looking my way.

There was just something about her, more than just the cute face and sexy figure. She was sweet and

The Teacher and the Virgin

confident at the same time. She was friendly, but never let anyone walk all over her. Both the way she acted and looked made her seem older, more mature, than she actually was. It was a sin for an eighteen-year-old to look the way she did.

It was a sin for a teacher to lust after a student. But she wasn't a student any longer. Yes, she was young as fuck, but she was legal and she was mine. I'd known it from the first day she'd sat down in my class and that little uniform skirt had slid up her pale thighs. I'd tried to behave, to ignore her, but then she'd started watching me, her eyes burning into me every damn day. She *wanted*. And even if she was too young, too innocent to recognize what she was feeling, I knew. I knew and I was going to be the one to give it to her.

I'd decided then and there she would be mine. I'd just had to bide my time all year until she was no longer my student.

I'd wondered how I would approach her, but that day last week and the note she'd passed with her friend Anne? It had been… fate. I'd wanted to jerk off all week at the thought of her eager to give me—me!—her virginity, but decided against it. I wanted to save up every drop for her. All my cum would be for Jane. I couldn't wait to fill her up, to watch as she tried to swallow it all, to see it slip from her broken-in ass and pussy. I'd never waste another drop inside a damn condom. I'd take her raw with nothing between us. Her virgin pussy would never know anything different.

Fuck, I'd assumed she might be a virgin still, but her note had confirmed it. She wanted me to be her first and I was going to do that for her. *Every* one of her firsts. I'd be the only one who touched her. The only one whose cock made that mouth open wide. The only one whose cock breached that tight little ass. The one who'd take her cherry. Her pussy, her ass, she was mine. Every innocent inch of her.

I was done waiting.

"So how's everything going with the bar exam?"

Fuck. I tried not to groan again, forced myself to push the dirty thoughts to the deepest parts of my brain. I shifted my head to the side and tried to put on my best smile. Liz, the school's music teacher, was looking expectantly at me.

"It's in a few months, isn't it?" she then asked, widening her smile.

I nodded my head and tried to think of something else to say to carry the conversation, but a familiar mop of blonde hair nabbed my attention from afar. Jane was huddled in a circle with Anne and a few other friends. They were wearing their graduation gowns, which was too long in my opinion, but the wind would blow against it from time to time to reveal their above-the-knee plaid skirts.

Fuck. I cursed inwardly again. My cock officially had a mind of its own. I shifted slightly to the side. I didn't want to be poking Liz or anyone else with my dick, and with Jane, I wanted to do more than poke.

"Fuck," I said to myself, shaking my head and laughing. My thoughts were betraying me, and I knew it was just futile to control my thoughts.

"Oh—" The look on Liz's face was priceless. She was three years older than I was, but acted much older than thirty. To put it bluntly, she walked around like she had a stick up her ass, and someone needed to get that stick out, but that wasn't going to be me.

"Sorry," I apologized. "I just remembered something I needed to do."

"Oh, what is it?" she asked, shifting her eyes away to look at the students and parents milling about.

Most of them were taking pictures and exchanging well wishes. I eyed Jane from afar. She was holding her phone in front of her and taking selfies with friends. I noticed she was the only one in her group who didn't carry a bouquet of roses.

Where were her parents? Had they left already?

These affluent, wealthy students had a lot of those —absentee parents. Well, the parents had to get the money from somewhere. The fifty-five-thousand-dollar annual tuition didn't pay for itself.

"Sorry, am I bothering you?" Liz asked when I hadn't said anything in the past two minutes.

Yes. "No, of course not." I said a little too quickly. "I mean…there's really nothing much to say about studying for the bar is there? It's in two months, so I'm just trying to take in as much information as I can. I'll be spending the summer with my face in the books."

Or between Jane's parted thighs.

"Well, I'm sure teaching Civics and Government helps."

Not really, but I nodded my head. "It does."

Jane helps, my consciousness said, and I realized I needed to leave before I could get a full-fledged hard-on for the entire world to see. "Excuse me."

I turned around, without saying anything more, and walked back to the main building, up the stairs to my classroom to wait.

For Jane. To make her mine. Finally.

Just thinking about her and reading the note she'd passed with Anne was enough to make my dick jerk against my pants. I placed the back of my hand firmly against my dick. Thank *fucking* God the building was completely empty. What I wanted to do to Jane was just for me. I would be the only one who'd see her body, the only one to hear her sounds. I'd take her how I wanted, where I wanted, including my favorite fantasy, bent over my desk.

On it with her legs spread apart.

On the floor. Under the table so she was kneeling between my legs, sucking me off as I sat in my chair. Against the cabinets.

The school supplies littering around would be a nice touch – that ruler to spank her.

She's a virgin, I reminded myself.

We'd have time for the wilder stuff later on. For now, even just thinking about traditional sex with *her* was enough to make me come in my pants. I tipped my head sideways and looked at the clock just above the doorframe. She'd be here any minute now, but my dick couldn't wait any longer. I'd been rubbing at it for a few minutes now. A few more strokes and I'd make a mess and I didn't want my cum anywhere but in Jane.

I couldn't fucking help it. Everywhere and anywhere I looked in the classroom, I was thinking of what I'd do to her.

There was a light knock on the door.

"Come in," I called.

The door opened and in came Jane.

With the summer sun high above in the sky outside, her cheeks were flushed from the heat. Though I couldn't help but notice they turned redder when she met my eyes. Her eyes – they were hesitant and expectant at the same time. She knew what was going to happen, but at the same time, she wouldn't know what to do.

I smiled at the thought. I would teach her everything and anything she needed to know, and I'd take my time. The longer the wait, the sweeter the fruit, and the expression couldn't be any more apt than with Jane.

She stayed rooted in her place, waiting for me to tell her what to do. Yes, I would be her teacher once again. I'd fallen in love with her over the last year, listening to her joke with friends, straining to hear her laughter. She was never cruel to her classmates or catty with the other students. She was classy, beautiful and extremely intelligent. And she was lonely. I recognized the look in her eyes, the need to belong.

She was mine, she just didn't know it yet.

"Close the door. Jane. And turn the lock."

3

ane

I DID AS I WAS TOLD. I SHUT THE DOOR, PRESSED THE lock, and with every second passing I felt more and more nervous and excited at the same time. Today was the day, the day I was going to lose my virginity to Mr. Parker. Just thinking about him made me wet, and I squeezed my thighs together when I felt my inner walls clench in anticipation. I'd fantasized about this so many times. Since that first day he entered class and introduced himself as our teacher, all I wanted was for him to take me.

When I heard the click of the door, I held my breath and waited for him to give his next instruction. He'd taped thick red construction paper over the long, rectangular window in the door. His room was on the second floor. Below us, on the football field, parents and former classmates milled around taking pictures, hugging grandma and making party plans. The fact that they were so close, but had no idea where I was or what I was doing made me totally hot.

No one could see in this room but the birds. I was alone with Mr. Parker.

I didn't know why, but I liked the feeling of being told what to do, especially coming from him. He felt stronger and more powerful when he ordered me around, and I loved the secure feeling that gave me. With him dominating me, I felt like I mattered, like he cared. I knew next to nothing about sex, even though I talked a big game and had watched loads of porn. When it came to the real thing, I needed someone to guide me and I was so happy it was going to be Mr. Parker.

As he leaned against the desk, he stared at me, took in the shapeless graduation gown. I immediately felt a surge of heat run through my veins with that stare. His eyes roamed my body, from my face to my legs, and I worried when he tipped his lips down into a frown.

What did I do?

"Take that off." He pointed his finger at the gown.

Hesitantly, I did as I was told and kept my eyes on him as the black material fell and pooled around my brown uniform shoes and ankle socks. Suddenly, the air around me felt hotter. I was literally just a plaid skirt and panties away from being taken. I wanted this, didn't I?

I did, I mentally reaffirmed myself.

But I didn't know what to do! What if I didn't please him? He'd had women, real women—not girls like me—what if I wasn't appealing to him with my shy ways?

Before I could back out, he pushed off the desk and moved closer to me.

"You've been a bad girl, Jane," he said, my name rolling off his tongue. "Passing notes in class…" I looked away, my nerves getting the best of me. My pussy wasn't cooperating though. My muscles *there* were contracting and relaxing again and again. "And writing about losing your virginity instead of listening to the exam review."

Slowly, he shook his head from side to side and I felt my stomach plummet.

I'd disappointed him.

"You want someone to take that pussy of yours for the first time?"

I bit my bottom lip at his question and managed to squeak out a tiny "no".

"I didn't hear you, Jane."

"No?" He stopped moving and I found my courage.

Now or never, Jane.

"No. I don't want someone to take my pussy." I licked my lips and stared at his. "I want you."

He was so close to me, just a foot or two away, and I

could see just a ghost of a smirk on his full lips. "You want me to take your sweet pussy?"

"Yes."

"Yes what?" I glanced up and saw his dark eyes were dilated and focused totally and completely on me. I was a virgin, but I'd had guys look at me like that before. Mr. Parker wanted me. He wanted me as much as I wanted him.

"Yes, sir. I want you to take my pussy," I said, a little more confidently than last time.

I froze up when I felt his hand graze my thigh at the hem of my uniform skirt. I held my breath as he brushed a little higher, then stopped.

"I need to teach you a lesson first," he said. Just like that, he moved away from me.

I whimpered, wondering what he was going to do. My heart beat frantically and I bit my lip as I watched him walk over to his desk and open his drawer. He took a ruler out and started to slap the end of it against the palm of his hand. Every sharp snap of noise made my pussy clench. By the time he turned back around to face me, I was shaking so badly I could barely stand. I'd heard the term *weak in the knees*, but never understood… until now.

"There," he pointed to the desk, then looked at me with those dark, piercing eyes. He'd never once looked at me like this in class. I gulped at the intensity of it. "Bad girls who break school rules need to be taught a lesson."

Internally, I was jumping for joy amidst the nerves. I realized I didn't need to worry so much. I needed to stop overthinking. I didn't need to worry about Mr. Parker regretting his decision and walking away. If he didn't want to have sex, he would've told me I'd been mistaken and asked me to leave. Hell, if he didn't want me, he wouldn't have ordered me to be here today, now, exactly one hour after graduation.

Yet here he was, and showing a different, sexier, and wilder side of him the students would never ever see. Only me.

"Are you going to spank me?" I asked, walking to the desk.

When he just stood there, I realized he was waiting. Putting my hands on the cool wood, I bent my torso over the desk.

He didn't waste any more time and walked to my side.

"Bad girls get spanked on the bare. Lift the uniform, please."

Oh my god.

Reaching back, I slowly lifted the hem of my plaid skirt, shimmying my hips as I did so that it rested up about my waist.

I turned my head and saw that he was just staring at my panty clad bottom, jaw clenched.

"No panties, Jane. If you're giving your pussy to me, that means it needs to be bare and available to me at all times."

His hands found their way to the elastic of my white lace panties and tugged them down so they rested just above my knees. I could feel the cool air on my bare skin, knew he could see *everything.*

The ruler came down with a crack and I startled. The searing heat of it had me gasping.

"Passing notes is not allowed."

He swung the ruler again. I hissed out a breath as it struck a new spot.

"What do you say to that, Jane?" he asked, striking again.

The sting was sharp and hot, but not overly painful. In fact, it only made me wetter. He had to be able to see the effects the spanking was having on me.

He dropped the ruler onto the desk with a clatter.

This time, when he spanked me, it was with his bare hand.

I gasped.

"Jane?"

"No, sir. I mean, yes, sir." I didn't know how I was to answer him. I'd forgotten what the question was as his palm stroked over my heated flesh.

"Do you like being over my desk like this? Punished by your teacher, you bad girl?"

"Yes, sir," I said. That was the truth and he knew it. I wouldn't be here otherwise. He wouldn't be spanking me otherwise.

"Do you like the idea that anyone might come in and see just how naughty you are?"

The Teacher and the Virgin

I hadn't thought about anyone else, only Mr. Parker. I squirmed on the desk, nervous all of a sudden.

"Mr. Park—" I began, but I was cut off when his finger slid over my slick folds, then started to circle around my clit. He started out slowly at first, the feeling building up inside me, until he started to pick up his pace. "*Please* finger me," I moaned and begged. "Please, sir." I wanted him inside me.

"Patience, Jane," he said, never stopping the movements of his finger. "Great things come to those who wait. Just leave it to me."

I closed my eyes and nodded my head, as he leaned forward, his chest against my back. We were now both bent over the desk. "Before you know it, I'll have my dick in you, pushing in and out and feeling everything inside you. But finger you? What a naughty idea. The first thing you'll feel in that virgin pussy will be my cock." To make his point, he ground his pants against my tender ass, all the while his finger pleasured my clit.

My moans grew louder as he continued to rub against me. I could feel the build-up inside me, like something great was about to happen.

I kept mouthing out "more", and he never once stopped moving his finger. My clit was swollen and sensitive beneath his attentions, my pussy lonely. It had never felt like this when I touched myself. I wanted *more*.

"Fuck me, *please*," I begged, when the feeling was getting too much to handle for a virgin like me.

"What did I say about patience, Jane?" he said, his free hand coming down on my bottom, the sting mixing with my need. He sounded both serious and teasing at the same time. "I'm in charge. This is my classroom, isn't it, Jane?"

I nodded my head.

"Are you the teacher?"

"No." I wouldn't know what to do, much less lead someone else. *Damn it, Jane.* I internally reprimanded myself.

"That's right," he ran a hand up and down the back of my bare thigh, making me shudder. "Because I'm your teacher."

"Yes, sir." The reply came naturally to my lips.

We were going to have sex – I just needed to wait. We'd get there, but I wanted it *now*. The heat in my pussy was just too much, and I felt like I was going to lose it.

"Good," he said, continuing to rub his fingers against me as he leaned forward so I could see his face. "Are you sure you want this, Jane? For me to take your virginity? Once we start, there's no backing out. You'll be mine."

Mine.

I nodded my head against the desk. "Yes." I said it again but louder this time. "Yes, sir."

"Perfect. Are you on birth control?"

He stopped when I shook my head. "No. I brought a condom."

He spanked me again. "You're mine, Jane. And I want to take you bare. I want to feel everything when my cock is buried balls deep inside you."

I whimpered at the idea of his cock entering me, skin against skin as he broke through that tight barrier. But I was also afraid. I wasn't ready for a baby. I wasn't ready for this.

His finger moved to the entrance of my pussy, circled it. "We're not having sex today. And we're not having sex with a condom. Ever. I don't want anything between us," he began. "You're going to the doctor tomorrow and get the birth control shot."

"Yes, sir." I nearly wilted in shocked relief. So that was it? This was some kind of tease? A test? What?

His finger moved away and he stepped back. I waited in place for a moment, then pushed up away from the desk. When I spun to face him, his eyes dropped to the apex of my thighs and I quickly pushed my uniform skirt back down before tugging at my panties.

"Those come off."

I glanced up at him as I was working them up, then gulped, changing direction. I slid them over one foot, then the other, placing them in the hand he held out.

I was achy and needy and so damn horny as I watched him tuck them into his pants pocket. My bottom stung from his punishment. I felt... chastised and I definitely learned one lesson. Mr. Parker was not going to let me get away with anything. I also learned that not coming was more of a consequence than a spanking.

There was a hint of disappointment stirring inside me. *So we weren't having sex today? Was he mad I wasn't prepared, that I'd told him we'd use a condom?*

But all my insecurities and questions flew out the window when he said, "There are other ways we can pleasure ourselves for now...so, so many more ways."

The sexy smirk on his face both unnerved and excited me.

Going around the desk, he pulled back his chair, sat down.

"I'll take your virgin mouth first, young lady."

He crooked his finger and as I came around the desk to join him, he undid his belt buckle. When I stood between his parted knees—him at my front and the desk behind me—his palm came up to cradle my cheek again, and I couldn't help but nuzzle it closer to him. His hand felt warm and rough, the hands of a man, and it made me feel protected.

A large part of me was nervous at what was about to happen. I'd watched enough porn to know he'd fill and fuck my mouth.

Slowly, I dropped to my knees before him.

"I've dreamed of you being right here. Open my pants."

I did as instructed as he continued to talk.

"I imagined you beneath my desk, your mouth on me, sucking the cum from my balls."

I moaned at the thought of doing that to him as the other girls sat at their desks and took their final exams. I wouldn't have a written test. My grade would come from oral work.

There was that smile on his face – the mixture of a grin and a smirk – but his eyes looked softly at me. I didn't need to worry and overthink so much. Just with the look he gave me, I knew no harm was going to come to me.

Hesitantly, my hands began unzipping his pants and my eyes stared at the thick bulge beneath. He didn't wear underwear.

"Jane..." The sound of my name brought me back to reality. "Are you alright?"

I blinked my eyes once and then twice and then looked up at the man before me through my lashes. My pussy was throbbing. I wanted – needed – to feel more, but we weren't having sex today. I couldn't believe I thought we were going to have sex with condoms. He was way more experienced than I could ever imagine, and I still couldn't believe he wanted to have sex with me. Just that thought made me feel hornier, if that was even still possible.

"Tell me what to do," was all I said, and his eyes softened all the more.

"Of course," came his response, and then, he squeezed my hand before he put it over the open zipper. "You're going to learn how to suck my cock like a good girl, aren't you?"

He breathed heavily when my hand started to rub up and down, and then, he took his cock out of his pants. I could only stare for a few seconds as I nodded my head. This was the first time I'd ever seen one in real life, but *damn*, his cock was huge, even for porn standards. He didn't notice my shell-shocked expression, or if he did, he ignored it. Instead, he wound my fingers around his length and started to move my hand up and down. Up and down.

I licked my lips. "Yes, sir."

"You can start with your hands before you use your mouth," he advised, words slow and interspersed with groans of pleasure.

With a slow nod, I continued to move my hand up and down the length of his dick before my mouth hovered just above the tip. I planted soft, quick kisses on his head and it caught me by surprise when it jerked every time I kissed and sucked slowly. I quickly felt more confident and started to take more of him into my mouth, deeper and deeper until I moved my hand away. The groan he elicited was music to my ears. He sounded like he was doing his best to keep quiet, but he just couldn't do it.

"Yes, Jane…" He said to me as his head fell backwards and his eyes remained closed. "That mouth of yours… you definitely know how to use it. I thought you were a good girl."

I didn't feel like a good girl. I was on my knees in my classroom with the broad head of Mr. Parker's cock touching the back of my throat. I wondered how far I could deep-throat him as I breathed through my nose. I'd make gagging noises from time to time, but he didn't seem turned off. It actually turned him on even more, if his hands taking fistfuls of my hair was any indication.

"Yes, Jane…that's perfect," he murmured, his hands guiding the movements of my head, up and down his dick. "You're fucking perfect."

Before I knew what was happening, I felt his dick twitch inside my mouth and then a flood of his cum overpowered me. Salty. It tasted like him. I froze on the spot as it inundated my mouth.

"Swallow it."

I did automatically, again and again to get it all down. When the flood stopped, I moved my head back and I could see some cum dripping off the tip of his still hard length. I quickly lapped it up and made sure nothing was left. When my eyes lifted to his, I could see Mr. Parker staring intently at me. He looked well sated.

"Shit, Jane," he began. "You were amazing."

Kneeling before him, I felt small. While I knew I'd pleased him, I worried I didn't compare to all the other women and their experience. "You're just saying that to—"

"No, I'm not." He shook his head, his eyes never leaving mine. "You followed my directions, and fuck… you swallowed while your mouth was still around my dick. Virgin or not, you're *very* rare, Jane."

I didn't know how to reply to that. For a virgin like me, his words felt like I'd just won the Olympics. I'd been scared and nervous the whole time. I hadn't wanted to disappoint him—I still didn't— and it was amazing to know I had pleased him. I could breathe now.

"And this was just you sucking me off." His face was a cross between exalted and confused. "I'm sure fucking your pussy will be amazing."

"I'm getting the shot first thing tomorrow," I promised.

I was sure I could squeeze myself in for a last-minute appointment at a nearby clinic. I was eighteen and didn't have to worry about the doctor telling my mom I was getting birth control. She probably wouldn't even care if I was being sexually active. Maybe, she'd be even proud that I was being safe.

"I can't wait," he said, taking a piece of paper from his drawer and scribbling something on it. "Here's my address. Meet me at my place tomorrow evening. I'll cook us dinner."

All I could do was nod, but deep inside me, the butterflies were aflutter in my stomach.

"Wear your uniform, but no panties."

Just another nod again.

"I'll check."

And with that, I stood up and headed for the door. "And Jane?" I turned my head to look at him, just as I had the last day of class. This time, I knew he wanted me. I had a belly full of his cum to prove it.

"Don't touch yourself. That pussy belongs to me. I didn't let you come on purpose. A spanking isn't the only punishment I'll give you if you're naughty. If you come on your own, I'll know."

My inner walls clenched as I wondered how I'd be able to make it until tomorrow night.

4

ane

I LIKED AND HATED THE FEELING OF THE NIGHT WIND brushing my bare pussy beneath my short skirt. I was the only person still wearing the school uniform. I'd graduated and was no longer a student. But I was Mr. Parker's student, and if he wanted me to wear the naughty schoolgirl uniform, I'd wear it.

Just as he ordered, I wasn't wearing any panties, and the moment I left my car and walked up to his front porch, I felt hot and cold at the same time, cool from the night yet heated with the thoughts racing through my head. A part of me was scared. It'd been drilled in my head never to talk to a strangers, much less go to their house. I shook my head at my own thoughts.

Mr. Parker wasn't a stranger. I'd been attending his class for the past year. I'd sucked him off the day before. If he was up to no good, he would've shown his true colors already. I pushed the negative thoughts to the back of my head; I knew I was just psyching myself out.

Getting the birth control shot earlier this morning seemed like a wake-up call, that this – losing my virginity – was really going to happen. I was a bit bummed out though when the gynecologist told me I'd have to wait seven days to be protected against pregnancy if I had sex. I made a mental note to tell Mr. Parker about that. He'd be able to wait… right? He didn't need sex asap, right? He wouldn't look for someone else…right?!

He opened the door before I could ring the bell.

"I heard your car pull up," he explained. At least I knew he was eager to see me.

He made a move to the side to let me in. "You better not be wearing anything underneath that uniform, young lady."

Just the deep command of his voice made me wet.

When I turned to face him, he'd closed his front door and leaned against it, arms crossed.

I realized he was waiting for me to show him.

Slowly, I pulled up my skirt, held the hem with my fingers at my waist. His eyes widened at the sight of my pussy, bare and wet for him. I didn't know why he looked so surprised, but he stared at it in such an intense and mysterious way that I couldn't help but think back to after graduation. Sucking him off had felt so good. I thought women did it just to please the men, but I would do it anytime without him even asking. It made *me* feel powerful, the way I'd been the one to make him come. Little young virgin like me had made Mr. Parker blow his load.

Everything about it – I just wanted more, the shape of his dick, the way it felt around my hand and lips and throat, and even the feeling of his cum flooding my mouth. The taste of it.

"Did you see the doctor?"

I tipped my head into a nod and started to lower my skirt, but the shake of his head stilled my hands.

"I want to look at my virgin pussy."

I cleared my throat and blushed, but answered his question. "The doctor... she um, said we have to wait a week."

He only nodded in reply and told me I could let my skirt drop. "Come."

He took my hand and let me in. His place felt like home. It wasn't as big as my parents' house, which really was a mansion, but it was more than enough for him. The living room was equipped with a high-tech computer gaming system, and right below his TV, there were numerous consoles waiting to be played. It wasn't the gadgets that made me feel hotter and wetter than I already was though; it was the furniture. I was thinking of all the places we could have sex, from the computer desk and three-seater couch to the dining table for four and the granite kitchen counter. My mind was running a marathon, and he was the only one that could satiate it.

"I promised I'd cook us dinner. That way, we can avoid the noise and the prying eyes."

"And the foreplay…we can't do that in public," I had to add. I'd been so quiet until now I didn't want him to think I was regretting coming over. It was all I wanted.

"Oh, Jane…" He shook his head; the smile was back on his face again. "I have so many things to teach you…"

I wanted to ask him questions, but he went into the kitchen. *Exactly what could I expect? We can do foreplay and sex in public?* I made a mental note to look for porn videos in public places. I realized there was tons I needed to educate myself on, but hey, if I was going to study, I'd pick sex education *any* day over Math or English.

The delicious scent of Italian distracted me and I went into the kitchen and watched Mr. Parker carefully pull a tray of lasagna from the oven.

"Mr. Parker, that looks delicious."

"Just call me Gregory," he said with a wink. "But don't tell your classmates that."

My heart jumped. I could call him by his first name? None of my friends could do that.

"Ex-classmates." I matched his grin with one of my own. "I graduated yesterday, remember?"

I watched Mr. Parker – Gregory – shake his head as he kept the smile to himself. "Of course. How can I forget what we did?"

I felt a surge of warmth all over my body, from my chest to my pussy. I didn't need to ask him to explain. We were thinking the same thing. That moment in his classroom was just too good to ever forget. I breathed out heavily; I didn't need to worry so much. He didn't look like he was going to run the other way anytime soon.

"Can I help with anything?" I asked.

A large part of me hoped he would say "no." I was almost useless in the kitchen since my parents hired a full staff to run the house, from cooking to doing the laundry and gardening. I didn't want to think it, but I suddenly felt embarrassed for living such a spoiled life. I hoped Mr. Parker wouldn't think differently of me if he realized I was spoiled and could do almost nothing around the house. "I can handle the drinks."

"Shh," came his quick response. "You're my guest. There's garlic bread in the oven. I prepared it a while ago for us. Just sit down and make yourself comfortable." I gave him a nod. "You can go to the living room and find something to watch. I'll be there in a sec."

"Okay." I knew better than not to listen to him. When Mr. Parker wanted something, he got it. Having me over wasn't an exception now that I was out of his classroom.

In a few minutes, he joined me with plates of lasagna and bread. My stomach grumbled when the smell wafted past my nose, and I felt my mouth start to water.

He placed the plates on the coffee table before he headed back to the kitchen. When I turned around to wonder what he was doing, he returned with a bottle of soda and two glasses in hand. He poured our drinks and then settled comfortably on the couch right beside me. Our thighs brushed against each other, and I couldn't help the way my heart skipped a beat and my nipples tightened. He just had that effect on me.

"Are your parents alright with you being out at night?" he then asked.

Being almost a decade younger than he was, my defenses went up. "I'm eighteen already."

He smiled at me, then glanced down at my body and replied with a murmured, "I know".

I calmed down at that before I said, "They're in Europe…have been for the past week."

"Hmm…I thought so." When I raised an eyebrow up at him, he continued, "Anne and your other friends had congratulatory flowers while…you…"

"Had nothing…I had nothing," I finished and watched as he nodded in agreement.

Before the mood could turn any more negative, he let out a cough and steered the conversation in a different direction.

"So what are your college plans?"

I widened my eyes, both at the fact that he was halfway done with his food and that he was asking me questions. Real questions, about me. Not about how wet my pussy was or if I was wearing a bra.

I thought he was just after sex with me, a virgin, so why were we actually talking? Not that I was complaining. I definitely wasn't. In truth, it made me like him even more. He actually wanted to talk to me, a girl who barely knew anything about the world. He didn't look down on me. *Could he get any more perfect?*

Over the rest of dinner, I told him of my plans to attend the local college. All the while, I maintained eye contact, realizing I'd never tire of looking at those caramel brown eyes.

5

regory

"Why do you want to go to the college here?" I asked, watching her as she took a sip of her soda, watching her throat work and remembering how she'd swallowed all my cum.

I was really trying my best to think with my mind and not with my dick, but it was damn near impossible. Knowing she wasn't wearing anything underneath that uniform skirt had me rock hard. I clasped my hands together and rested them over the growing strain.

I didn't want her to think I just wanted her just for sex. Sure, that was a large part, but Jane was so much more than sex. She was mine. Knowing she wanted to stay in town for school only made it even more official.

There were so many things to learn and know about her, so many layers to unravel and I was willing to take the time to do it.

"What do you mean?" she responded, wiping her mouth with a napkin.

"The school is small. You're a very smart girl, Jane, not only in my class." I took a quick pause. "If you wanted, you could go to the best schools anywhere in the country."

I watched her, noting the way her brown eyes widened. She held a sharp intake of breath, released it, and stayed silent for a few seconds. She looked like she was nervous; the expression on her face was of worry as she wrinkled her forehead. I'd never seen this side of her – genuine concern.

She was the girl who knew how to carry herself and seemed like she'd never had a problem in life. She'd strutted along the school's hallways with that bright smile and the sensual sway of her hips. Seeing her now – a different side – all the more piqued my interest.

"I'm not sure if I could do it…"

I moved one hand to her knee and squeezed it, pressing her to continue. She looked at me for a second before she tilted her head away.

"I've never left home. I don't know the first thing about living independently."

She stopped for a second, the hesitation evident.

The Teacher and the Virgin

She stuck her bottom lip out and moved her eyes downwards. She looked ashamed.

I immediately crinkled my eyebrows. An ashamed Jane was a sight I never wanted to see. It didn't fit her. She had so much potential for that kind of feeling.

"I've never had a job. I don't even do my own laundry. I can't cook. Everything's been done for me, whether I wanted that or not. Sure, my parents will still pay for everything, but they've never been around." She raised her hands up in the air and then dropped them. "I don't know. I just have no interest in leaving here. I'm content staying in town for college."

"Good," I said. She was mine and I wasn't having her go to a school two time zones away. I wouldn't hold her back if it was her dream, but it wasn't. Her damn parents hadn't given her confidence to spread her wings. While she was content to go to college, venturing far was not exciting for her. Why should it when she didn't have a secure and loving home life?

"Good?" she repeated, biting her lip.

"Because your pussy belongs to me, remember?"

She nodded and looked down. Her cheeks flushed prettily.

"Do you still want that? Do you still want me to be in charge of you?"

She looked up quickly. "Yes, sir." Her voice was adamant.

"Good girl."

I watched as she preened by the praise.

"It seems there are many lessons I have to teach you, don't I?"

Her cheeks turned darker when she realized I was talking about fucking. Yes, I'd teach her exactly what I liked and I'd show her just how she'd love it, too.

"Yes, sir," she said again.

Tucking her hair back behind her ear, I said, "They will include punishments, Jane. Are you prepared to be tossed you over my knee and spank you to learn a lesson? Fill your ass with a plug so you remember who's in charge?"

Her eyes widened at that. Yes, I'd put a big plug in her ass so she'd remember who she belonged to, if required. Or, if I just wanted to. The more she knew how things would be, the better.

"You'll punish me if I cook and burn dinner?" she asked, clearly worried.

"I'll punish you for it if you were forgetful because you were playing a game on your phone."

She nodded.

"I'll punish you if I find out you were texting and driving. Or if you don't have your phone with you when you go out. Or if you flirt with any college boys."

She smiled then. "College boys? I don't want a boy. I want... you."

"You want a man who knows what he's doing, don't you?"

She nodded, glanced at me with those innocent

eyes. "I like it when you take control," she admitted, then glanced down at my cock.

She was still shy when it came to her sexuality, but she was getting better at owning it. She was starting to make eye contact more often, and she was always an eager student when it came to listening, making sure she heard and followed everything I said.

"Oh, you do?" The only response she gave was a nod, but that was more than enough. "Do you like it when I tell you what to do? When I tell you how to suck my dick?"

"Yes," she whispered, and I watched as she closed her eyes for a second.

"When I punish you for being a bad girl?"

"Yes."

"When I reward you for being good?" I put my hand on her bare thigh and slid it upward beneath the hem of her uniform.

"Hm—" I watched her take in a deep breath before she answered back, "Yes, I love it."

"Did you touch yourself last night when you were alone in your bed? Did you spread those thighs and put your fingers in that virgin hole? Did you make yourself come?"

She shook her head vehemently.

"Well, you've definitely been a good girl then, following everything I say," I began. I hooked a finger under her chin and tipped her head up until our eyes met. "And do you know what good girls get?"

Her cheeks quickly turning red. "I hope… I hope I get to come."

"You'll find out," I said with a mischievous smile, as I slowly pushed her back onto the couch, so her back was comfortable against the cushion.

By the time I was done with her, she'd be a wet mess in my hand…or mouth. I couldn't wait for it – seeing the look of euphoria from her first time being eaten out.

I dropped to my knees on the carpet in front of her. I didn't hesitate to pull her ass closer to the edge of the couch before I spread her knees apart. I sucked in a breath when I saw the lips of her pussy glistening wet and taunting me. Inhaling, I breathed in her sweet scent.

"You're dripping wet," I growled, her cream even coating her thighs.

She moaned and lifted her hips when I slid my fingers through her desire. I wanted to take her slowly, almost painstakingly. I wanted her to beg desperately for me. For what I'd give her. No one else would make her this way.

I wanted her to moan and scream as loud as she wanted. I couldn't care less if her noises kept my neighbors awake. She was eighteen. Everything we were doing was legal, but in this case, legal didn't mean safe and boring. I almost chuckled loudly at the thought. I had a lot of things in mind, and none were safe or boring. There was a lot in store for her.

Bringing the wetness to my mouth, she watched as I licked my fingers clean. Her taste was sweet and tangy and my mouth watered for more.

I glimpsed her virgin hole with her lips parted and wanted to rip open my pants and sink into her. It wasn't time yet. Even if I could claim her now, I wouldn't. There were so many firsts with her I had to claim before I took her cherry.

"You like that?" I asked with a smile, the pad of my thumb rubbing circles over her clit. I felt a surge of confidence run through me when every soft touch I laid on her had her moving her hips. I couldn't wait for the finale, and my dick was telling me to get on with it.

Jane spread her legs wider. Her pussy capped with only a narrow strip of pale hair. She kept it tidy, trimmed, and maintained, and I just couldn't help but think that every second with her was full of surprises.

For a virgin, she certainly seemed to know what to do and how to act. My mind flitted instantly to the day before. She'd never even seen a dick in real life, but she sure knew how to suck mine. But the bashful looks and the soft, barely audible voice gave it away though – her being a virgin.

"Mr. Parker—" she moaned, eyes shut tight.

"That's right, you'll call me Mr. Parker when you're wearing your uniform, when you're my student," I told her. "I want to hear that when you're begging me for the dirtier, naughtier things I'm going to do to you."

A moan and then two came out from her lips, as her head fell onto the cushion and she arched her back.

"Undo your blouse and show me your breasts."

Her hands came up to the tiny buttons and undid them, parting the sides so that her pert mounds were exposed.

I tsked her. "No bra, Jane. Did anyone else see your hard nipples through that thin blouse? Did anyone else see those pert tits bob and sway as you walked?"

"No sir," she said as I cupped one and brushed my thumb over the tight tip. It was a perfect handful, not too big, perhaps a B cup… if she wore a bra. They were high and perky, just as a young lady's should be.

She gasped at one gentle pinch.

Perfect. Seemed my little student like a little pain with her pleasure.

As I played with her breasts, I lowered my head and put my mouth on her. Finally.

She was slick and sweet and I could eat her pussy for hours.

But I'd kept her on edge since the day before. She'd been spanked and I'd played with her clit before she sucked my cock. Then I'd left her hornier than ever. Now, she was so primed a flick of my tongue on her clit set her off. She writhed and screamed as her cream coated my lips.

The sound of her orgasm almost had me coming. Her thighs had clamped around my head and they'd quivered as she came. Her breathing was ragged and I

The Teacher and the Virgin

knew when she touched herself it had never been like this.

No, she'd come all over my face.

"Please," she begged.

"What do you need, young lady?"

She was sprawled lewdly on my couch, her uniform skirt bunched up about her waist, her legs parted and her pussy on display, all hot pink and swollen, dripping onto my leather couch cushion. Her pert tits were visible with her prim blouse parted, the pale skin glistening with sweat. She was every schoolgirl fantasy I ever imagined.

"More," she breathed.

"More what?" I asked. "Use your words and tell your teacher."

"Your cock. Please. I feel… I feel empty."

I'd longed to hear those words from her lips. With a gentle touch, I swirled her entrance. "Your pussy's off limits. No cock in that hole."

She whimpered her disappointment.

"I know it's hard, but doctor's orders. I've already claimed your mouth." Moving my finger lower, I circled the crinkled rosebud of her ass.

"If you want my cock, then I'll take this hole next. Has any boy ever touched you here?"

She tensed, but her head thrashed from side to side as I circled and pressed against the tight hole. "No."

"Then this will be tonight's lesson. Taking my cock in your ass."

"B-but—"

"You're wearing your uniform, young lady. You're going to be my good student aren't you, Jane?"

She opened her eyes and I saw they were blurry with passion, but filled with a wariness that only came with innocence. She looked down at herself and tugged her blouse closed, although it did nothing to make her look any less erotic.

Besides seeing her and defiling her in her schoolgirl outfit made me hot as fuck, it was also a symbol of her role. My student. Mine.

"Yes, sir."

"That's right." Using her cream to ease the way, I pressed the tip of my finger into her back entrance. She moaned at the slight invasion before I retreated, stood and scooped her up into my arms.

"Good girl. That virgin hole's mine, too, and I'm taking it right now."

6

ane

I NUZZLED MY HEAD AGAINST MR. PARKER'S NECK, AND he felt so, *so* good. His flesh was warm against mine, his arms tight around me. I felt warm and protected, all because of him. He bound up the stairs, still carrying me bridal style, and when we reached the top landing, he turned to the left and walked towards the end of the short hallway.

He kicked the door closed behind us and my heartbeat sped up when I saw the king-sized bed in the middle of the room. *This* was actually going to happen – anal sex.

I'd watched that kind of porn, but I couldn't

imagine why people would actually do it. Wasn't my pussy more than enough for him?

Why would horny people need to find a second hole?

Mr. Parker wanted it though, had even slipped the tip of his finger in me. It hadn't hurt, but it had been uncomfortable and... weird. And good, if I admitted the truth. But his cock? It had been in my mouth so I knew how big it was, but there?

Mr. Parker's eagerness for it made me interested. He was the experienced one. He knew I'd like it; he wouldn't do it otherwise.

I'd tried sticking a finger in my ass once before after watching porn, and I didn't like the feeling. Would this time be any different, now that I was going to do it with someone much more experienced? Maybe, I did anal fingering wrong. I *hoped* I'd been wrong.

Mr. Parker threw me on the bed and I bounced once and squealed before I moved my body higher towards the headboard.

"I want that skirt up about your waist, young lady. Show your teacher your pretty pussy and ass."

He propped his hands on the edge of the bed and watched as I wriggled the skirt back up, my breasts bouncing as I did so. He then crawled closer until he hovered over me. His hand started to brush my skin softly, up and down and up and down my outer thighs, then skirting inwards.

"You're so fucking wet, Jane," he whispered against

my ear, as I kept my eyes closed. "I love everything about you. Your round, supple breasts, your pussy that's always wet for me, and that tight asshole that's going to soon be all mine."

Reaching over to his nightstand, he opened a drawer and pulled out a small bottle of lube and tossed a small egg shaped *thing* on the bed.

Snapping open the top of the lube, he dribbled some onto his fingers, rubbing them together to coat them liberally.

I bit my lip as I watched.

With his other hand, he picked up the egg and pressed a button. I could hear the vibrations and when he placed it directly over my clit, my hips bucked.

"Ugh-!" I moaned in shock when the vibrations worked my already sensitive clit, and I had to close my eyes tight as waves of pleasure inundated me. I started to hump his hand, thrusting my hips forward as my pussy clapped against the palm of his hand. Everything was just too much.

"Mr. Parker, finger me *please*," I begged desperately, but I already knew what answer to expect.

"No," he said quickly, giving a little swat to the inside of my thigh. "I'm going to lead." He pulled the egg away. "You bad girl. You know nothing goes in that virgin pussy but my cock."

I was ready to come again, twice in the span of minutes, and I loved it, until he took the vibrator away. He'd said there were worse punishments than a spanking and he was right. I was writhing with need and he was holding my orgasm from me.

"Up on your hands and knees. Yes, just like that. Go down on your forearms, angle your ass up. Yes."

I wiggled my hips.

"Such an obedient student. When I want your ass, you'll get in this position."

He didn't touch me, only waited. I turned my head and looked over at him.

"Yes, sir," I said finally.

I watched as he brought the lube up behind me and felt the cold liquid splatter out of the bottle and dribble down over the hole he was going to soon claim. His coated finger was there, swirling and pressing in. Soon enough, it slipped inside. I curled my back away as he pushed his finger deeper, then retreated. Was this what it would feel like with a finger in my pussy? Those inner muscles clenched with anticipation. It was just his finger inside my ass, but it just felt so, *so* tight.

He started to fuck me with that single digit and the feeling was completely different from that time I'd tried to finger myself in the ass.

"You wanted to be fingered, young lady, didn't you? How do you like today's lesson so far?"

I closed my eyes, just letting myself feel Mr. Parker's movements inside me. It wasn't long before he started to move faster, his finger pushing in and out before adding a second, then a third.

I was so full I clenched the sheets, groaned at the

slick stretch. I was going to come, just from this since he'd teased me with that damn vibrator.

"Please," I whimpered.

"Are you ready for my dick?" he asked, splaying his hand on the center of my lower back. I felt his domination, knew he had me just where he wanted me.

I nodded my head and my nipples brushed against the blanket.

I squeaked out a "yes."

My eyes remained closed as his fingers continued to move and assault my ass. A part of me was nervous, the other half excited, at the idea of his dick entering me from behind. I bet none of the other girls were getting their ass fucked. They'd all said Mr. Parker was the hottest teacher in the school, but I was the only one who'd get him.

Just the feeling of his fingers moving in and out was already more than enough. I couldn't even begin to imagine what his dick would feel like. It had to be bigger than his fingers. I'd soon find out.

He pulled them out, and I opened my eyes when I heard the sound of his belt and jeans coming undone. I heard the splattering of more lube coming out of the bottle, and I began to shiver as I waited for him.

"Patience, Jane," he said softly, his voice deep and strong still. "I'm getting my dick all slick. I don't want to hurt you. We'll take it slowly. I'll guide you through everything and give you the best experience you can ever have." I nodded my head and hunched my back when I felt his tip teasing my entrance.

At that moment, heart skipped a beat. We were having a hot and passionate moment, but my heart felt calm, relaxed...and wanted. He sounded like he cared for me, like he didn't want to hurt me, like this wasn't just a student-and-teacher role play. He sounded like he was truly concerned for me and the experience he was giving me, and I couldn't help but let my feelings for him grow. He wasn't just the experienced teacher whom I wanted to lose my virginity to; I wanted to spend more time with him now, get to know him better, have him become a larger part of my life.

"Hm-!" I squeaked when he began to push his dick in. He kept a strong hold on my hip, making sure I wouldn't pull away when he would push in more. I gripped the blankets to distract myself from the feeling of his full dick trying to push its way inside my tight ass. I couldn't explain the feeling. It didn't hurt as he began to stretch me open; it felt good, but at the same time, the feeling was both familiar and unfamiliar. I couldn't explain it.

"Don't overthink, Jane," he said, as he gave my shoulder a kiss. "I can tell you're stressed and nervous. Relax and take a deep breath. Let it out and push back. Good."

I did as instructed and felt his broad head pop inside me. I heard him suck in a breath at what just happened, and it was music to my ears when he breathed, "Fuck."

I couldn't help but wiggle my hips and he took it as a sign to work his way in, and when he finally was, he started to thrust in and out. At first he took it slow, letting me get used to the feeling. As he continued to push and pull in and out of my ass, he reached around and cupped one breast and pulled me closer until my back was flushed against his chest. He pounded me from behind, and I loved the feeling of his body right behind mine. I felt safe and protected, like no harm was coming to me, like he would protect me from everything outside our own little world. Even when he was doing the dirtiest, most wicked of things to me.

"You like that, Jane?" he asked, and I nodded.

"Yes, sir."

"I'm going to go faster now. Hold on."

Another nod from me. He kept his promise and began to pick up his pace, moving his hand from my breast to my clit. It was then I finally opened my eyes and saw stars.

"Oh, Mr. Parker..." I couldn't help but moan, biting my bottom lip to stop myself from screaming. "This feels so *fucking* good..."

He gave my ass a slap and then another one, working my ass from both from his hand and his dick. "You're a Catholic school girl. You're not supposed to curse."

I replied with a louder moan this time. He

continued to assault my ass, and I was letting him do it all too willingly. I wanted this. I wanted more. I wanted him, and to pass the message, I moaned louder and heavier until they crossed the boundary and turned to screams.

"Yes, Mr. Parker! That feels amazing!"

"Hmm…" I heard him, as he gave my ass another slap. "Who knew a prim young lady like you would like it in the ass?"

I couldn't hold back anymore. His fingers pressed against my clit, and I could only close my eyes and scream at the euphoria.

"Mr. Parker," I moaned his name. "I'm gonna cum. I'm gonna cum…I'm gonna…"

"Cum for me, Jane," he said, his tone both caring and demanding. "Let go."

He thrust even faster now, his fingers moving in circles against my clit. I squeezed my eyes tight and breathed out heavily. I felt my nerves relax a bit, and it was then that I was able to let go. I felt the whirlpool peak and break, and before I knew it, my pussy was flooded with my own juices and I knew his fingers had to be coated.

He thrust deep one last time and held himself still. He shouted his own release and I felt his cum spurt hot and thick deep inside me.

Slowly but surely, he pulled his dick out of my ass, and I felt that there was an empty hole inside me, both literally and figuratively.

But then, I smiled automatically when he pulled me closer to him and laid me on my back on the bed. I felt his hot cum slip from my used hole. I no longer had a virgin ass. The slight burn, the cum, were proof.

He planted a kiss on my lips. Our first kiss.

"I'll be right back," he said, and I nodded in response. He went to the bathroom and came back with a warm washcloth, which he used to carefully clean between my legs. "You were amazing. Would my little student like to spend the night here with me?"

"Yes," came my quick reply. "No one's home anyway."

No one was home, yes. But I didn't want to leave his side. I wanted to spend the night with him.

7

regory

"My parents don't give a shit."

Not a lot of things scared and shocked me. I could sleep and snore through horror movies. I'd jump out of a plane for just the thrill and fun of it. I'd eat disgusting insects, be it a dare or not. My friends would prank me and try to get me to break my cool and calm façade, but they always failed.

Except for Jane.

Hearing those words leave her mouth made me suck in a breath. I met her eyes and kept the contact, looking right at her. Her lips were pursed together, as her eyes remained searching mine for a reaction.

The Teacher and the Virgin

What could I say?

That this Sunday had been one of the best days of my life? That I wouldn't be able to sleep later because I'd be thinking about... everything? We didn't do anything extraordinary even, not today and not even during the days before. Jane had stayed the night in my place one more time after that first night she slept over, that night I'd claimed her ass.

We did everything, from cuddling to oral sex, and now, I always teased Jane about how giving me blowjobs was her new hobby. She'd initiate and do it out of her own accord.

She woke me up twice by sucking me, and after, we'd just spend the rest of the day cuddling. She'd undo my jeans and pull them down while I was trying to get some chores done around the house. I'd stopped wearing boxers to make it easier for her.

She'd even tried to do it to me in a public park, but I told her we'd try that in the evening when there were less people. I wouldn't have anyone else see Jane on her knees.

I'd made a mental reminder to follow through with that.

I'd yet to fuck her pussy, to finally take her virginity. Waiting the seven days was hard, but I'd shown her all the other ways to pleasure each other.

But now, I couldn't keep Jane out of my mind. She'd done something to me, and I wasn't complaining. I'd never complain when it came to her. These past few days, we'd spent tons of time together, and I was starting to realize that she was everything I wanted in a partner and more. I was getting to know her, the woman underneath that shapely body, and I was dying to find out more.

For her age, Jane was mature, both physically and emotionally, yet the youthful energy was obvious, especially in bed. Or on the kitchen table. Or up against the front door.

She was always wanting to please me and make me happy, be it in or out of the bedroom, but at the same time, she still spoke her mind. The women I used to date always ended up saying "no" more than "yes". They weren't adventurous and would rather stay in and have sex unless I took them out to upscale and fancy restaurants. With Jane, she was up for anything. She knew how to be both boring and fun, and even that already made her a cut above the rest.

"I care about you," I said when minutes of silence passed. "You're one of a kind, Jane, and it's a shame your parents don't see that."

"I—"

I froze in my seat when her voice cracked for a split second. We were in my living room after a whole day of exploring the city. We'd gone to the local museum and library, and for lunch, I'd taken her to this new café a friend of mine owned, and she was able to meet him. Since she was mine, I wanted to show her off. Not many eighteen-year-olds could start and carry a conversation with people over a decade older, yet Jane did it effortlessly. She was young, yes, but she was exquisite. I didn't give a shit what people thought. She'd be on my arm for events and reunions with friends. She'd easily fit right in.

Goddamnit, I internally cursed.

This wasn't about just being physically attracted to her and teaching her everything she needed to know about sex. I wanted her before, during, and after sex. I wanted to hang out with her more and take her out. I wanted her in my life. I'd known it from the start. I wasn't giving her up.

"What's wrong?" I asked, wrapping an arm around her shoulders and pulling her close to me. "You look worried."

"I'm scared you'll leave me once we've had real sex."

I almost broke out laughing but held it in. I knew Jane would take that kind of reaction the wrong way. It was just funny to me how, while I knew she was never going anywhere, she was worrying that I'd leave her.

If only she knew...

It was then I hooked a finger under her chin and tilted it up, so I could stare at her.

"You're mine, Jane," I began. "How many times do I have to tell you?"

She gave a slight shrug. "Maybe a few more."

I grinned. "Perhaps you're more of a hands-on learner."

With a gentle push, I forced her onto her back. With

one knee on the couch and a foot on the floor, I levered myself over her, tugging her so she was spread before me. I liked her wearing flirty skirts and this moment was why. I just had to toss up the short hem and her pussy was bare for me.

"Yes, Mr. Parker. Perhaps you need to show me."

She shifted so she could pull her t-shirt over her head, her bare breasts swaying as she settled on her back once again.

As I lowered my head to one plump nipple, I murmured, "You a very eager pupil."

Jane

"THEY'RE BACK." IT WAS THE FIRST THING I SAID WHEN he opened the door. He was in sweatpants and t-shirt, and the sight instantly made me horny even if I was feeling down. "I don't want to stay there tonight."

Mr. Parker immediately knew what I was talking about. My parents – they'd just gotten back from Europe. They'd returned with a mountain of souvenirs, from designer clothing to Swiss chocolates and the finest wines from France and Spain. They were all for me, even the alcohol, but after they'd said their "hi's" and apologized for missing my graduation, they

The Teacher and the Virgin

excused themselves and went to their home office. Mom needed to catch up with emails, and dad had a business dinner with some corporate partners. In a second, the mansion was back to being empty, and I felt lonely. After spending every day of the past week with Mr. Parker, the difference between the feeling of being alone and having someone to spend the day with was as clear as night and day.

Mr. Parker and I talked about meeting at eight tonight, but I went to his place a couple hours earlier. Why wait when there was nothing to do in the empty mansion? Besides, it'd been exactly a week. We both knew what tonight entailed, and I'd assumed he'd want me at his house sooner rather than later. It was time for him to take my virginity. He'd kept his word, nothing had gone into my needy pussy. Yes, he'd eaten me out and fucked my ass, but he'd kept my pussy as virgin as could be, ready to be stretched open first by his bare cock. During the drive, my imagination went wild.

I was already thinking about the dirty things I was going to say to him, how I was going to remove the tight-as-a-glove dress I wore. I was playing out the possibilities of later in my head. Would I keep my heels on or off? Maybe, I could ask that in a naughty way. My thoughts were racing, and it was a miracle I even got to his place in one piece.

"I haven't cooked dinner," he said to me, but that was honestly the last thing on my mind. I wanted to eat something else. Ever since that first time I'd given him a blowjob, I found the beauty in sucking dick. His dick. When he was in my mouth, I owned him. I was powerful and beautiful and more important, irresistible.

It was so much fun to do, and the shape of his tip and the length of his shaft was definitely a sight I could stare at all day and night. He'd tease me regularly that sucking him was now my new hobby. I'd laugh him off every time, but deep down, I knew he couldn't be more right. "Come in, Jane. Sorry," he apologized quickly. "I've been studying for the bar exam the whole day. My mind's burnt."

I entered his house and followed him into the living room. He sat down first and patted the empty space beside him, but *fuck*. The sweatpants and the even thinner t-shirt only made me feel hornier. If we started a movie, there'd be no doubt I wouldn't last through it. My eyes flew toward his cock where the length was outlined in his sweats, and I sucked in a breath. I wanted to have sex right then and there. I'd been waiting a full week, and I felt like I couldn't wait any longer. I wasn't going to tell him that outright though. I wasn't going to throw myself at him.

Because I loved it when Mr. Parker took charge, and tonight, I wanted him to take charge as he took my virginity.

I just needed to prod him, so I didn't sit next to him. Instead, I stood directly before him.

The Teacher and the Virgin

With a smile on my face, I began to wriggle out of my skintight dress. I'd move my ass left and right to get the spandex to ride up my hips. I held the hem with my fingers and pulled it over my body, and when my dress covered my face, my smile turned into a smirk when I heard him elicit a groan. I wasn't wearing any underwear—just the way he liked me—and in a second, I was full-on naked in front of him. To add to that, I'd gone to the salon yesterday to get a full wax. My pussy was bare and free from any hair, and I clenched when I felt a surge of heat burning inside me.

"Fucking…" Mr. Parker breathed as he stared at me. I threw the dress onto the floor and walked closer to him until my legs touched his knees. "Jane…" he groaned again, running a hand through his hair. I could see the hunger burning in his eyes.

"It's been a week," was all I said. I didn't even need to say that to let him know what was on my mind.

"Not here," he said, and in a second, he was on his feet and he'd swooped me up in his arms. He raced up the stairs and then kicked open the door to his bedroom. Then, he dropped me onto his bed. "It's your first time. We're going to do it the right way."

"It's right as long as I'm with you," I courageously said, letting him know what I felt.

"Such a good little virgin."

I saw his eyes soften a bit before he moved them down to explore my body. I felt a shiver run up my spine when he began to trace a finger over my skin, from the curve of my neck and down the valley between my breasts, then lower still, over the newly bare pussy lips.

I inhaled sharply when his finger stopped right at my entrance. My eyes widened when he planted just one kiss over my pussy. Then, he rose up to kiss me on the lips. I tasted myself on him. The moment was so emotional and intense. He wasn't rushing to take me.

He didn't undress and stick his dick in right away, just as I wanted. By the look on his face, I could tell he didn't want to rush tonight. He wanted to take me, yes, but he wanted tonight to be special, too. It was going to be my first time. It was going to be *our* first time. There were no repeats or refunds for firsts. I could tell what was on his mind with the way he acted and moved above me – caring and loving he was.

And I couldn't help but blurt out, "I love you."

My heart instantly froze when those three words left my mouth. Silence enveloped the room, and I was thinking of taking back what I said. He stayed deathly quiet, and I felt like my heart was going to crack the moment one of us moved. I turned my head to the side to look away, but right when I was about to do so, he moved his head down towards my pussy and began planting soft kisses at my entrance.

He licked and laved my pussy, his lips swiping my folds and his tongue trying to push deeper. He sucked once and then twice, all the while his hand continued to rub up and down my thigh while the other cradled my waist. There was nothing rough and eager about the way he moved, and it was relaxing and calming, and it was just what I needed. He continued to kiss and suck my pussy, and I savored the moment with eyes closed and my mind blank and empty. I was *in* the moment, and it was the only place I wanted to be.

I arched my back off the bed when his tongue started to play with my clit, and I let out a series of moans when I could feel the ember growing inside me. The whirlpool was building up again, and he knew what was about to happen because my moans then turned into screams, and those screams turned louder with every minute passing.

"Gregory..." I breathed, when I felt myself about to tip over the edge. "Please..."

In an instant, he was off me. My eyes widened, questioning, but he only smiled at me as he began to take off his sweatpants.

"Another lesson, naughty girl. What do you call me?"

I wiggled my hips. "Mr. Parker, please."

He pulled the t-shirt over his head and threw it across the room. Settling back between my parted thighs, his full erection teased my entrance, and I could see some pre-cum drip from the tip.

"Please, what?"

"Please fuck my virgin pussy."

I'd gotten brazen in sharing what I wanted.

"How?"

"With your fingers. With your big, hard cock."

He settled back on his heels and began to stroke himself. "With this?"

I bit my lip and nodded. When he arched a brow, I said, "Yes, sir."

"It's going to fill you right up, open you wide, go deep inside you, isn't it?"

My inner walls clenched at his dirty words.

"You won't be a virgin anymore. You'll still be my good little girl, won't you?"

I nodded, reached down and ran my fingers over my clit.

He tsked me and gripped my wrist, placing it up by my head and not letting it go.

"Such a needy, naughty girl. Do I need to spank your ass first before I fuck you good and hard? Fill you with my seed and mark you as mine?"

I arched my back. "No, sir."

He released my wrist and sat back again. "Hook your hands behind your knees and pull them back. Good. Wider. Yes, like that. Now I can see your virgin pussy and well claimed ass. It's all mine, isn't it?"

"Yes, sir."

Placing his hand by my head, he settled over me. I felt a finger at my entrance, circling, but not entering.

"Please," I begged, gripping my legs nice and wide.

"We're going to finish together, alright?" he said, his eyes staring at mine before they moved to look at how we were almost joined. His tip was caught around the lips of my pussy, and I was dying to have my hands on his ass and push him all the way in, but I stopped myself from doing that.

That would make me a bad girl, and Mr. Parker would punish me. While I loved it when he gave me that extra attention I craved, even when bad, it wasn't what I wanted tonight.

He'd take me hard and fast, but I wanted this to be slow and intimate. I loved him. I didn't want sex tonight. I wanted to make love.

"I'm going to start slow, Jane," he then said, beginning to push inside. His words had tamed, his voice more soothing than scolding. "It's going to hurt a little bit, so I'm going to ease you into it."

I nodded my head and shut my eyes, as I felt him move deeper. Felt his broad head stretch me just as he'd promised.

"That's right, baby. They're we go, Jane. You can take me…all of me."

"Yes," I managed to groan, eyes still closed as I was trying to get used to his size. My pussy was wet, and I could feel his dick gliding smoothly inside me. Still, it felt tight as if my inner walls were being stretched to their limits. He looked at me and I held his gaze. All at once, he thrust deep, took my virginity with his big dick, just as he'd promised.

I groaned at the bite of pain, the way he filled me up.

"I can't go any deeper, Jane," he said. "You feel fucking amazing."

He remained still, just for a bit, letting me adjust to him, just as he'd done when he'd taken my ass for the first time.

And then, he started to move, slow and steady. I laid still as he pushed in and out of me. I wanted to thrust my hips. His dick glided effortlessly inside my wet pussy, but it was just *so* tight; I felt a little bit strained. I couldn't explain the pain. It slightly hurt yes, but it was the welcomed kind. It was the kind of pain that I didn't want to go away, and I made my feelings known by releasing my hold on my legs and cupping and squeezing his ass as he continued to thrust.

"There we go, baby," he said, beginning to pick up his pace, and I found myself automatically smiling at the feel of his dick moving in and out of me. I couldn't believe what I'd been missing. *Fuck*. I was suddenly hungry and desperate for him, and I couldn't help but start to rock my hips and match his pace.

"Fuck…you're such a good student," he said, moving faster. "You get an A. That's it…"

He cupped my breast. I moaned. He began to rub my clit, and I squeezed my vaginal muscles, thanking the Kegel Gods. He groaned loudly, almost beast-like, when I did that.

"Fucking hell…" he roared, as I stayed clenched.

"Yes…yes…" I moaned, as he continued to move inside. "Yes…yes…" The whirlpool was reaching its end, and he knew it was so, as I'd begun screaming again.

When I opened my eyes, I found him staring right at me. His eyes told me what I'd been dying to hear from him. *He loved me.* I could feel it. He didn't need to tell me outright. Everything he'd done was for me. He took charge because he knew I needed guidance. He spent as much time with me as possible the past week because he knew I was truly alone despite all the material things and friends I had. He started me slowly with sex tonight because he didn't want to hurt me. I didn't need to hear those three words from him. I could feel it.

"Oh, God...!" I moaned loudly when I felt myself shivering and writhing underneath him. My juices mixed with his inside my pussy, and I could feel the bed sheet become moist underneath me. He continued to pump in and out of me, slowly now, our cum dripping to the bed with every pull of his dick. I let out a series of breathy sighs when he finally came to a stop, and I was a wet mess beneath him.

"You're amazing," he said, as he rolled off me and laid down on my side. Then, he splayed an arm across my stomach and pulled me flushed against his torso. "I love you, too, baby. I love you, too."

His words surrounded me like a warm, perfect bath as I fought back tears. My parents were the only people who'd ever spoken those words, and even then, they'd been rushed and automatic. A reflex, like saying hello or good-bye when one answered the phone.

But this felt different. Real.

I rested my head on his chest as his hand rubbed up and down my waist. I found myself suddenly sleepy and tired. There was no doubt I'd have the best sleep of my life. Content, sated and well fucked.

EPILOGUE

Jane, one year later...

I COULDN'T WAIT TO GET HOME – TO HIM.

The past weeks had been super stressful. And that was an understatement. I'd been pulling all-nighters to meet project deadlines and find time to study for exams. I was going crazy...and becoming ugly due to stress. I didn't care about wearing make-up the past few days. Everyone in the university was a walking zombie, and no one took the time to look the least bit presentable.

And here I thought the high school workload was bad.

I made an exception today though with the flirty

floral dress and a pair of strappy wedges. I'd even taken the effort this morning to apply some make-up and curl my hair and did a retouch just a few minutes ago, the moment my last exam ended. With no more exams and projects to think about, I could finally relieve some stress, and in the best way I thought possible – sex.

I rushed home to Gregory's – our – house and made sure to keep within the speed limit. Calling him Mr. Parker was saved for the bedroom, and Gregory was how I usually called him now, behind 'babe' or 'baby'. I'd moved in with him a few months ago, and I couldn't believe we'd been together almost a year. None of our friends or family thought we'd last the summer. But I knew. I knew the first time he touched me that I wanted more. Not last? *Ha!*

I stepped on the brake pedal the moment I pulled into the driveway. I turned the engine off before I rushed to the front door, leaving my books, laptop, and bag behind. I couldn't care less about them now that all my deadlines were done.

I rang the doorbell twice before a mischievous smile and knowing caramel brown eyes greeted me.

"You're home early. I was thinking you were going to celebrate with your friends…" Those ever-familiar eyes roved my body from head to toe before they went back up to my breasts and then my eyes.

"I thought of another way of celebrating," I said with full confidence. "Mr. Parker."

I grabbed the ends of my dress and lifted it up. His

eyes widened at the sight of my underwear-free pussy, bare and wet for him.

"Don't tell me you took your exams without any panties..." He couldn't help the groan that left his lips, and I noticed the growing bump beneath his jeans.

I took a step and then two closer to him and whispered, "I did, Mr. Parker. That's why I finished the exam earlier than everyone else. I was thinking about you, not the test, and my pussy was getting wet in class."

"You're a bad girl, aren't you?" he said, his firm, strong hand resting against my bum. "I think I have to teach you a lesson."

"I don't think so, Lawman," came my response, coupled with a teasing smirk. He'd passed the February bar exam in just received the results last week. He was a lawyer now, with a fancy new office downtown. That office had a very nice desk, a desk we hadn't christened yet. I grinned up at him. "You're not a teacher anymore. And besides...I think I was a good girl today. For finishing the exam well before time was up? And I managed not to leave a single question blank."

He managed a low, raspy chuckle before his hold tightened around my ass. With one swift tug, he pulled me inside the house – our home – and slammed the door closed behind us. In seconds, I was pushed up against the wall and my dress hiked dangerously above my hips. Only air separated my pussy from his hand as his fingers slowly closed the distance between us.

"I still have things to teach you, don't I?"

"Yes, sir," I replied.

"So baby…have you been a good girl or bad girl?" he whispered, warm breath massaging my burning skin, as his fingers rubbed up and down my entrance. "One gets dick in the pussy, and the other gets fucked in the ass."

I couldn't help but let the breathy moan escape my lips. Which was which?

Did I care?

No. I didn't. "Either. As long as you're the one fucking me."

He pushed two fingers inside me as he held me pinned to the wall. My body bucked as I begged him for more.

He worked me with his fingers, his mouth locked to my throat, his free hand holding my wrists pinned above my head as I came all over his hand.

When I opened my eyes, it was to find him watching me, a look I'd never seen on his face. Serious. Intent.

"I love you, baby."

God, I knew it. I knew it, but he rarely said the words. He showed me, though, every time he touched me, I felt it. "I love you, too."

"Marry me."

I gasped, shocked as he worked his fingers in and out of my body slowly, so slowly working my clit.

The Teacher and the Virgin

"You're mine, Jane. This pussy is mine. Your heart is mine. Marry me."

I nodded, biting my lip as an aftershock of pleasure whipped through me. Emotion flooded me as I lifted my lips for his kiss. "Yes, Mr. Parker. Yes."

His pants dropped to the floor and he filled me up, right there against the wall. Rough and raw and just the way I wanted him.

Forever.

Read on for special BONUS BOOK: Lip Service by Jessa James.

WANT MORE? READ HIS VIRGIN NANNY

Maybe it's crazy. Maybe it's wrong. But don't care. I need him.

HIS VIRGIN NANNY- CHAPTER 1

abe

I HADN'T EVEN MADE IT THROUGH THE FRONT DOOR OF my best friend's house and my dick was hard. It wasn't because of him. It wasn't just Greg who'd answered the door, but with him were two young women. One was his new love interest, Jane. And although she was pretty, it was her friend who made me feel like a little kid who'd just seen tits for the first time. Not only did she get my attention, but my dick's, too.

When Greg told me he had someone in mind to babysit my niece, I was expecting some socially awkward teenager who'd gotten the short end of the puberty stick. Wasn't that how babysitters were portrayed in movies, complete with the glasses, bangs, and forehead of pimples?

I looked at *her* – Mary – from head to toe. Yes, she had the bangs, but her emerald eyes were scot-free of any glasses, and every inch of her gorgeous skin looked flawless. It didn't even look like she was wearing make-up, it was so subtle, yet she could turn heads. It did mine.

I blinked my eyes a couple of times and instantly glanced at those D-cups. I hadn't meant to, but they were pointing right at me. When I brought my head up, I could see Mary's smirk curved very slightly into a small grin. I was good at reading people; Mary liked the way I was looking at her. The way I was reacting to just the sight of her. I should behave, I knew it, but I couldn't control the urge to ogle her. What I *really* wanted was to *touch*, kiss, taste that creamy skin, put a flush on her cheeks as I made her whimper with need, fill her with my dick and watch her curves bounce as I thrust hard and deep. God, I was screwed and I hadn't even gotten past the doorway.

I was an animal for thinking about her in such a way, but she was gorgeous, with her oval-shaped face and high cheekbones…and sexy, too, with slender legs, a full ass, and an endowed rack. Her hair was long and dark, almost black, framing her perfect face, pouting pink lips and green eyes that sparkled with innocence and desire at the same time. The look made my entire body go on high alert, my cock turning rock hard.

This was a woman I could teach, protect and thoroughly enjoy introducing to the world of sex and heat and breath-stealing pleasure. I had no doubt she was innocent. She might have fucked a high school boy before, but there was no doubt she'd never been with a man. With most women, I usually had to pick between innocent and sexy. I couldn't haven't both. But Mary? She was perfection. I wanted her.

Which was stupid. She was eighteen. Jane's best friend. The fucking babysitter. And just that fast, I felt like a schmuck. A real asshole. But this was insta-love or some shit like that because she was going to be mine. Mary was mine, she just didn't know it yet.

"Hey man, you alright?" Greg's words brought me back down to Earth.

"Yeah," I easily recovered from my daydreaming/salivating. "So, you're Mary?"

Our eyes maintained contact – my azure ones meeting her green ones. She looked at me with her bottom lip pouting slightly, and her arms were crossed, one over the other, to rest below her breasts. With the additional support, her cleavage deepened, and so did her smile. I didn't know which to look at.

"It's nice to meet you…"

"Gabe," came my smooth reply, as I extended my arm to shake her hand.

The Teacher and the Virgin

"That's so formal," Mary responded. She took a step, then two, closer to me, opening her arms wide and brought me into a hug. I was too surprised to hug her back, too caught up in the feel of her breasts pressing against my chest.

"Don't tell me you hug your teachers that way?" I asked, my tone teasing. When she pulled away, she raised an eyebrow at me and turned to face Greg. He taught Civics and Government at the nearby private school for girls, and Mary had been his student. She just graduated and wanted to earn some extra income before college started in the fall, and it just so happened I was looking for a sitter.

I'd promised my sister I'd look after Ashley, her two-year-old, during her six-month deployment to the Middle East, but I still needed to work. As an architect, construction sites weren't exactly the place to take a two-year-old. When I stole a glance at Mary, I couldn't help but think she was heaven-sent. Not only did she look like an angel, but she was one, too. I wouldn't know what I'd do without a sitter. I loved my niece, but I couldn't be with her twenty-four/seven. Besides, I had no mothering instincts whatsoever.

"Isn't anyone hungry yet? I'm starving!" Jane exclaimed. Greg had met his match with her, and by the satisfied look on his face, he'd put her in her place: beneath him. Or maybe on his lap. Or on her hands and knees. I wasn't interested in Jane, and my thoughts shifted to thinking about Mary in those positions. With me.

"Did Greg wear you out? Is that why you're hungry?" Mary teased her friend and I choked, shocked. Yeah, I'd had similar thoughts, but those words from sweet Mary?

I switched my glance from Jane to Greg repeatedly, and I could see Jane's cheeks start to turn red. That was the kind of shit I liked to give Greg non-stop, and that was exactly why we were friends. That Mary was joining in on the fun made her twice as interesting. I just hoped I could get *her* to blush like that.

I couldn't help but stare at the girl…or rather, woman. Woman – that was what I meant. For a couple of eighteen-year-olds, Mary and Jane looked mature, all grown-up – in an *extremely* good way. Their clothes were tight, hugging perky breasts and tight asses, but Mary knocked me dead with a megawatt smile that make my dick stir. Which was not good, not right now. Not on Greg's front stoop. But a man who didn't stare at them was probably gay. It was no wonder Greg was nuts for Jane, that he got some all the time.

When he first told me he had the hots for an eighteen-year-old, I gave him shit. Greg was handsome, and he knew how to work the beard. He was even a lawyer, or would be once he passed the Bar exam. He was a catch. Women his age would flaunt themselves at him, but according to him, there was just something about Jane, something that actually made him get into a committed relationship. Last time I talked to him, he was thinking marriage—which was nuts. He hadn't asked Jane yet, but she'd practically moved in with him. Her family was usually off traveling the world, so devoting her time to Greg appeared to be an easy choice. And if I had a woman like her in my bed every night...

"You're just jealous you don't have a hot, young girlfriend...and sex-on-demand," returned Greg. Yeah, he'd read my mind.

"That was gold, man." I clapped my friend on the back. "You got me there. No sex-on-demand, and I'm done with the one-night-stands."

"Hmmm…" My head moved to look at the owner of the soft voice. Mary was looking at me with a curious brow raised before she curved her lips up into a small smile. Then, she looked away and wrapped an arm around Jane's.

"I heard we're having steaks," she said. "I'll help get things ready."

"All the food's been prepped," Greg told her. "I just need to grill the steaks. Come on in."

Greg and Jane, hand in hand, led us toward the kitchen.

Mary said, "Thank you for inviting me over for dinner, Mr. Parker. Your home's lovely."

"No, thank *you*," came his response before he glanced at me for a second. "You'll be doing Gabe a huge favor by looking after his niece this summer."

"No problem, I *love* children," she replied, her tone almost cooing, as she met my eyes. "How often does she need to be watched?"

Before I could open my mouth to speak, Greg was quick to say, "Before you two talk business and start being boring, let's eat first. Potatoes and salad are ready, and the steak will come in a few minutes."

With a series of nods, the three of us took our seats. I sat beside Mary, our legs touching beneath the table, and I couldn't help the sudden stirring feeling inside me.

Damn.

Damn. Damn. Damn. I was in trouble. My dick was getting a zipper imprint just because our thighs were touching.

That was all I thought throughout dinner. When Mary tied her ebony hair up into a ponytail, exposing her nape, I couldn't help but hitch my breath. I tried my best to be as subtle as possible. When Mary opened her luscious, red lips to take a bite of the steak, I used all my willpower not to wonder what they would look like around my dick. When she easily contributed to the conversation with her light, feminine voice, I discovered she was smart and witty as well as beautiful. Everything about her – I just wanted to experience more. *Hell*, I fucking wanted to taste her. All of her.

"How's your steak?" she asked.

Out of courtesy and a little nudge from my dick, I glanced at her, more like stared, actually. Her lips

The Teacher and the Virgin

curved up into a small smile, and she turned so her upper torso leaned toward me. My eyes glanced down to look at her cleavage. I couldn't help it. I was only a man and fuck... it was lush and she was more than a handful. I clenched my fists so I wouldn't cup her in my palms and feel how heavy they were, see how they overflowed over my fingers. When I looked back up, her smile had turned into a curious smirk. It was as if she was taunting me.

There was no doubt she was flirting. I'd had experience with women trying to grab my attention; I knew most of what they stored in their bag of tricks, and it looked like Mary was playing the same game. I shook my head subtly. I didn't want to think about it too much. She was eighteen years old.

When I'd been eighteen, I was an awkward, lanky kid who didn't know how to flirt. The girls back then were the same. We were all naïve and knew close to nothing when it came to attracting the opposite sex. From the looks of it, Mary had no problem with getting *my* attention. Hell, I wasn't going to be able to forget her. No, her scent, her eyes, her curves were burned into my brain. She had me, and my dick, wrapped around her little finger.

"Gabe?" she called out my name when I still hadn't responded to her.

"It's great. Want a bite?"

Automatically, I sliced my meat, forked the small portion, and held it up right in front her mouth. I saw the way her eyes widened at my gesture, surprise painted on her face. Looking at her, I couldn't move my head away. From her high cheekbones and full lips, every part of her complemented each other to form a masterpiece. She finally leaned forward, opened her lips, and had a taste of my steak. When the medium-rare meat touched her tongue, she closed her eyes, savoring the taste, before she opened them again. Holy fuck, the sound she made. Part moan, part gasp, I wanted her to make that sound again, but when she came all over my cock.

This was an intro to a fucking porn video.

Especially with the way she looked and moved – feminine, youthful, and yet calculating – it was hard not to want to know more about her. She didn't act or speak or look like an eighteen-year-old. My dick didn't care about her age. She was legal, she was gorgeous, she was smart, she was into me. She was mine.

As dinner continued and conversation lengthened and turned lighter and more informal, I was starting to see her as someone who didn't let herself be dictated by her age. She talked about her plans for the future; she was going to take up early education since she wanted to be a pre-school teacher. It was noble, and I saw myself wanting to know everything about her. She wasn't just the gorgeous and sexy Catholic schoolgirl that made my dick hard, although the thought of her in her plaid uniform skirt was making my cock press painfully against the zipper of my jeans.

The Teacher and the Virgin

She was a complex human being who wanted more in life than just to coast through. She had hopes and dreams and was going to move across the country for college.

"Are you ready for the big move yet?" I asked her. Jane had just come back from the kitchen to take the strawberry cheesecake from the refrigerator. She cut a slice each for us, handed the plates over, then took her seat beside Greg. All eyes turned to Mary.

"Hmm…" There was a tinge of hesitation in her voice. "Not really. Honestly, I don't want to move, and I planned to go to the local college, but my mom keeps telling me that specific college is the best for a degree in education. And that's the only school she'll pay for."

I frowned. "I'm sure you can talk to her about it," I offered, tilting my lips up into a warm smile which she returned. Her mom sounded like a bitch if she was dictating where her daughter went to school. Withholding money for any other place? That was blackmail.

I didn't want to see her upset and this conversation was clearly ruining her mood. I decided to change the subject. "I'm just thankful I found you to look after Ashley. I promise she's well-behaved."

Mary was quick to shake her head, obviously disagreeing with what I just said. "She's two. She shouldn't behave all the time. It's not a problem at all. I swear. I love kids, and I've already planned to take her to some parks and the science museum. I'm sure there's also more than enough time to take her to the zoo."

"Save the zoo for the weekend," I quickly piped up. "The three of us will go together."

I didn't miss the sneaky smirks that surfaced on Jane's and Greg's faces. My friend looked at me and raised his eyebrow. Yeah, I was just as fucked as he was. No, I hoped to be getting fucked as much as he was. Soon. I just had to get Mary naked and beneath me, show her she was mine.

Jane started shaking her head as she looked from me to Mary. I knew what they were thinking. They put us together as employer and babysitter, but had they done a little matchmaking, too? I didn't care if they thought that. I just wanted Mary any way I could get her.

"We'll leave you two," said Greg, taking the dinner plates off the table and leaving the cheesecake. "I'm sure you want to come to an agreement before she starts sitting for Ashley. Jane and I will be in the kitchen."

Yeah, matchmaking. Worked for me. I had to remember to buy Greg a beer the next time we had a guy's night. I owed him one.

When the two of them left the room, I turned to face Mary, to give her my full attention. Our knees touched and she stared up at me with a mix of a smile and a smirk. With our closeness, I couldn't help but

The Teacher and the Virgin

inhale her womanly scent, and I knew right then and there that I was a goner.

She might be my new babysitter, but there was no *fucking* way I'd be able to keep my hands off her.

Get His Virgin Nanny now!

GET A FREE BOOK!

Join my mailing list to be the first to know of new releases, free books, special prices and other author giveaways.

http://freehotcontemporary.com

JESSA JAMES BOOKS

Bad Boy Billionaires
Lip Service
Rock Me
Lumberjacked
Baby Daddy

The Virgin Pact
The Teacher and the Virgin
His Virgin Nanny
His Dirty Virgin

Club V
Unravel
Undone
Uncover

Jessa James Books

Beg Me
Valentine Ever After

ABOUT THE AUTHOR

Jessa James grew up on the East Coast but always suffered a severe case of wanderlust. She's lived in six states, had a variety of jobs and always comes back to her first true love – writing. Jessa works full time as a writer, eats too much dark chocolate, has an iced-coffee and Cheetos addiction, and can't get enough of sexy alpha males who know exactly what they want – and aren't afraid to say it. Dominant, alpha-male insta-luv is her favorite to read (and write).

Sign up HERE for Jessa's Newsletter:

http://jessajamesauthor.com/mailing-list/

www.ingramcontent.com/pod-product-compliance
Lightning Source LLC
LaVergne TN
LVHW011847060526
838200LV00054B/4208